# Count to 20 with Macy

Written and Illustrated by:

Christine Kuschewski

This book is dedicated to Macy's second family. Will, Melissa, Austin, Eli, Toby and Kona, thank you for loving Macy! Thank you for watching her when I'm gone. She loves you all so very much!

Macy is learning how to count. She loves to count whatever she can find around the house. Today she is at Toby and Kona's house counting objects. They have boys so there are a lot of toys. Let's see what Macy finds to count.

"Look what I found! " shouted Macy. She had a medal hanging around her neck.

Can you count 1 medal?

1 one

"Look! I found a couple of watches! " shouted Macy.

Can you count 2 watches?

2

two

"Look what I found! " shouted Macy. She found some fun balls.

Can you count 3 balls?

**3**

**three**

"Look! I found some yummy desserts! " shouted Macy.

Can you count 4 desserts?

4

four

"Look! I found zoo animals! " shouted Macy.

Can you count 5 zoo animals?

5

five

"Look what I found! "
shouted Macy. She found
some eye glasses.

Can you count 6 eye
glasses?

6

six

"Look! I found these cubes! " shouted Macy.

Can you count 7 cubes?

**7**

**seven**

"Look what I found! " shouted Macy. She found some candy dispensers.

Can you count 8 candy dispensers?

8

eight

"I found the pop its! " shouted Macy.

Can you count 9 pop its?

9

nine

" I found all these socks! " shouted Macy.

Can you count 10 socks?

10

ten

"Look what I found! " shouted Macy. She found some hearts.

Can you count 11 hearts?

11

eleven

"Look ! I found the stuffed animals! " shouted Macy.

Can you count 12 stuffed animals?

**12**

**twelve**

" I found all these tubes! "
shouted Macy.

Can you count 13
tubes?

**13**

**thirteen**

"Look at all these puzzle pieces! " shouted Macy.

Can you count 14 puzzle pieces?

**14**

**fourteen**

"Look!  I found some beautiful flowers! " shouted Macy.

Can you count 15 flowers?

15

fifteen

"Look at this! " shouted Macy. She found some building blocks.

Can you count 16 building blocks?

**16**

**sixteen**

"Look what I found! " shouted Macy. She found some shapes.

Can you count 17 shapes?

**17**

**seventeen**

"Look what I found! " shouted Macy. She found a group of cars.

Can you count 18 cars?

**18**

**eighteen**

"Look! I found all the balls! " shouted Macy.

Can you count 19 balls?

19

nineteen

"Look! I found dinosaurs! " shouted Macy.

Can you count 20 dinosaurs?

20 twenty

"All that counting has made me tired. Let's take a nap." said Macy, as she lay down next to Toby.

Christine Kuschewski has been a special education teacher for 22 years. She loves teaching children how to read. Her love for books and education has led her to writing children's books.

Christine and Macy live in Arizona. Macy loves to spend time with her best friends, Toby, Kona and their family. Macy is a 7 year-old Bichon Frise, Poodle, Maltese and Shih-Tzu mix. Everyone who meets Macy falls in love with her. Together Christine and Macy enjoy spreading love to the world.

Made in the USA
Middletown, DE
10 November 2022

14552348R00029